Brave Lion, Scared Lion

Brave Lion, Scared Lion

Joan Stimson

Illustrated by
Meg Rutherford

SCHOLASTIC INC.
New York Toronto London Auckland Sydney

Look out for
Big Panda, Little Panda,
A New Home for Tiger,
and Swim Polar Bear, Swim!
also by Joan Stimson and Meg Rutherford.

ISBN 0-590-03195-3

Text copyright © 1997 by Joan Stimson.
Illustrations copyright © 1997 by Meg Rutherford.
All rights reserved. Published by Scholastic Inc., 555 Broadway, New York, NY 10012, by arrangement with Scholastic Ltd.

12 11 10 9 8 7 6 5 4 3 2 1   8 9/9 0 1 2 3/0

Printed in the U.S.A.   14
First Scholastic printing, March 1998

On a faraway plain, near a cool water hole, lived twin lion cubs. Their names were Jake and Jasper.

As they grew, the brothers would wander to the water hole and admire their reflections.

"What a brave lion I am!" cried Jake. And he growled
and he prowled with pride.

But Jasper kept quiet. Because Jasper was timid and shy.
And sometimes he felt scared. He felt scared when Jake
chased him up a tree and then he looked down.

He felt scared if Great-Uncle Jiggly Jowls bellowed
when Jake bit his tail.

And Jasper *shivered* when Mom took them down to the river. And warned them about crocodiles.

"I wish I could be brave like Jake," sighed Jasper.
But Mom was always ready with the same reply.
"Good heavens! There's more to being brave than
showing off."

Then she would give Jake a playful push.

And lick Jasper gently behind his ears.

One day Jake and Jasper set off for the water hole. "Don't be long," Mom told them. "And stay well away from the river."

But, when the cubs had drunk and played and admired their reflections, Jake wanted to do something different.

"Come on," he called to Jasper. "I'm going to count the crocodiles."
By the time they reached the river Jasper was worn out and worried.

Jake was disappointed. "There's not a crocodile in sight," he grumbled. So he decided to show off.

"Don't!" pleaded Jasper. "It's dangerous and it's time to go back." But Jake was already dancing from rock to rock and singing, "What a daring lion I am!"

Jake was still enjoying himself when a rock by the far bank shifted and stirred. First a pair of eyes appeared. And then ... a huge mouth.

"Watch out," cried Jasper. "It's a crocodile!"
Jake froze in his tracks. He was too terrified to move
a paw.

Because suddenly, every rock looked like a crocodile to Jake.

Jasper was terrified too. But he leapt to Jake's side. And tugged at his tail.

The tug brought Jake back to his senses. And with a squeal he hid behind Jasper.

Just at that moment Mom arrived on the bank with Great-Uncle Jiggly Jowls.

"What a brave lion you are!" bellowed Great-Uncle Jiggly Jowls as Jasper led Jake to safety.

"And what a naughty lion you are!" Mom told Jake.

All the way home Mom was angry. Because she'd been anxious.

Later on, at supper, Mom was not quite so angry.
But at bedtime she spoke sternly to Jake. "Now what
have you learned today?"

"Not to play by the river. And that there's more to being brave than showing off," mumbled Jake. "Exactly," said Mom. And then she tried to explain.

"We all get scared sometimes. And it takes a really brave lion to overcome his fear and act with courage." Jasper wriggled with embarrassment.

I wonder if she'll still be angry tomorrow, thought
Jake, sleepily.

But, as the sun went down, Mom licked Jake gently behind his ears. She gave Jasper a playful push.

And when the cubs snuggled closer, she said exactly
the same thing to each of them.
"What a special lion you are!"